God Gave Us Sleep

by Lisa Tawn Bergren   art by Laura J. Bryant

WATERBROOK
PRESS

God Gave Us Sleep
Published by WaterBrook Press
12265 Oracle Boulevard, Suite 200
Colorado Springs, Colorado 80921

Hardcover ISBN 978-1-60142-663-5
eBook ISBN 978-1-60142-664-2

Text copyright © 2015 by Lisa Tawn Bergren

Illustrations copyright © 2015 by Laura J. Bryant, www.laurabryant.com

Cover design by Mark D. Ford; cover illustration by Laura J. Bryant

Published in the United States by WaterBrook Multnomah, an imprint of the Crown Publishing Group, a division of Penguin Random House LLC, New York.

WaterBrook and its deer colophon are registered trademarks of Penguin Random House LLC.

Library of Congress Cataloging-in-Publication Data
Bergren, Lisa Tawn.
  God gave us sleep / by Lisa Tawn Bergren ; illustrated by Laura J. Bryant. — First edition.
    pages cm
  ISBN 978-1-60142-663-5 (hardback) — ISBN 978-1-60142-664-2 (electronic) [1. Sleep—Fiction. 2. Bedtime—Fiction. 3. Christian life—Fiction. 4. Polar bear—Fiction. 5. Bears—Fiction.] I. Bryant, Laura J., illustrator. II. Title.
  PZ7.B452233Gom 2015
  [E]—dc23
                                        2015009353

Printed in the United States of America
2015—First Edition

10 9 8 7 6 5 4 3 2 1

Special Sales
Most WaterBrook Multnomah books are available at special quantity discounts when purchased in bulk by corporations, organizations, and special-interest groups. Custom imprinting or excerpting can also be done to fit special needs. For information, please e-mail SpecialMarkets@WaterBrookMultnomah.com or call 1-800-603-7051.

This book is dedicated to all
the mamas and papas of little cubs
who are praying for a good night's sleep!
Hang in there. It gets easier. We promise.

—LTB & LJB

"Little Cub!" Mama called. "Time for bed!"

"Awww, Mama," Little Cub said.
"I don't want to! We're building an igloo."

"I see that," Mama said. "You can start again in the morning."

"Okay…," said Little Cub,
dragging her paws toward the house.

"Are the twins asleep?" she whispered.

"Yes," Mama said. "They've been asleep for an hour already."

"I don't need as much rest 'cause I'm bigger."

"That you are. But all cubs need a good night's sleep."

"Even you? Even Papa?"

"Even us. God gave us work time and play time, and rest time too."

"Why does he want us to rest?"

"It's how he made us."

"Why? I think playin' is a whole lot more fun than sleepin'."

"God gave us rest so we have energy for our day,
and patience to enjoy it. And," she said, her voice
hushed, "so we have quiet time to listen to him.

Now, into bed with you, Little Cub.
It's time for a good night's sleep."

Little Cub knew it was time for sleep, but she wasn't quite ready.

"Can I have a glass of water?" she asked as Mama tucked her in.

"Yes," sighed Mama.

"Now I kinda hafta go to the bathroom."

"All right," Mama said, "but *hurry.*"

"Can you read me a story?"

"Sure. Choose your favorite."

"Can we read one more story? *Pleeeeaase?*"

"Okay, just one more."

"Aren't you gonna pray?"

"Of course," Mama said, touching her nose to Little Cub's.

"For a good night's *sleep*."

Mama was almost out the door when
Little Cub said, "Um…Mama?"

"Yes, Little Cub?"

"What if God doesn't give me a good sleep?
What if I get one of those bad, scary dreams?"

Mama turned and knelt by her bed. "We should
pray for good dreams. For a good sleep."

And then, they did just that.

"No matter what happens tonight, Little Cub,"
Mama said, "remember that God is the Maker
of everything in our world, including our
imagination—where our dreams come from.
He can give you a good sleep."

"If you say so…"

"I know so," Mama said. "Trust him and think
about how he keeps us safe, like the biggest, best
bear you ever met. Think happy thoughts. Got it?"

"Got it."

"Good. Sleep tight, Little Cub."

Mama closed the door, and Little Cub flipped over.

And flopped over.

And wrestled with the covers.

She couldn't sleep
for very long.

"Good morning!" Mama said.
"Did you have a good sleep?"

"Uhhh…"

"Uh-oh. Did you have bad dreams again?"

"Naw. You said to think happy thoughts,
so I thought about the igloo.
But then my mind was too busy!
All I could think about was what I wanted to do today."

Mama let out a deep breath. "Oh, that *would* keep a cub's
mind busy. Have some breakfast, then out you go."

After she ate, Little Cub raced outside and worked hard
on her igloo with her friends. But as the day
went on, she got grumpier and grumpier.

She yelled at the pesky otters.

She fought over the shovel.

She walked off in a huff when Bonnie the Bunny
wouldn't let her open the gate first.

"Everyone's makin' me so mad!"
Little Cub grumbled, slamming the door behind her.

"You might be feeling cranky because
you didn't get a good night's sleep," Mama said.
"God gave us rest as part of our daily rhythm."

"Rhythm like a song?"

"Yes.

Work and rest, play and rest, work and rest, play and rest,"

Mama Bear said,
dancing with her.

"That's how it's
supposed to go."

Little Cub dragged through dinner…and dragged through dishes…and when Papa said it was time to go to bed, she didn't complain.

After they tucked her in and prayed for good dreams, Little Cub said with a yawn, "I'm glad that God gave us sleep. I'm *tired*."

"Us too," Mama said, kissing her nose.

Then together they prayed for a quiet mind, happy dreams, and a good sleep.

Little Cub closed her eyes and felt
the edge of sleep, like the best
of blankets covering her.

Soon she dreamed of the
most awesome iceberg
slide in the Arctic.

And she dreamed of riding
on a caribou sled through
the mountains.

And she dreamed of flying up
and among the Northern Lights.

Until she woke up to a beautiful new morning.

Stretching, Little Cub looked outside
and thought about how she couldn't
wait to be with her friends.

Even Bonnie and the pesky otters!

And she was glad, so glad,
that God gave her a
good night's sleep.